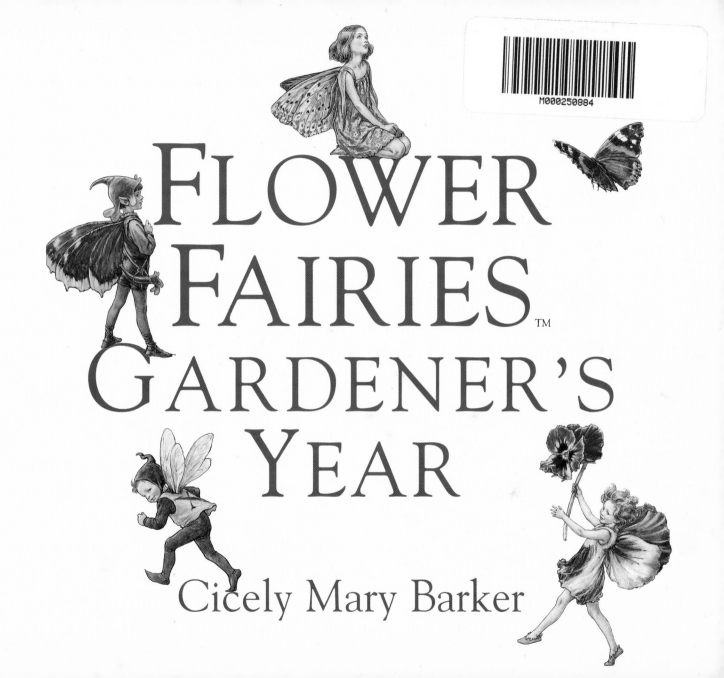

FLOWER FAIRIES™
GARDENER'S YEAR

Cicely Mary Barker

The reproductions in this book have been made using the most modern electronic scanning methods from entirely new transparencies of Cicely Mary Barker's original watercolours. They enable Cicely Mary Barker's skill as an artist to be appreciated as never before.

FREDERICK WARNE
Published by the Penguin Group
Penguin Books Ltd, 27 Wrights Lane, London W8 5TZ, England
Penguin Putnam Inc., 375 Hudson Street, New York, NY 10014, USA
Penguin Books Australia Ltd, Ringwood, Victoria, Australia
Penguin Books Canada Ltd, 10 Alcorn Avenue, Toronto, Ontario, Canada M4V 3B2
Penguin Books (N.Z.) Ltd, 182-190 Wairau Road, Auckland 10, New Zealand

Penguin Books Ltd, Registered Offices: Harmondsworth, Middlesex, England

First published 2000 by Frederick Warne

1 3 5 7 9 10 8 6 4 2

Text copyright © Jennie Hook, 2000
Original illustrations copyright © The Estate of Cicely Mary Barker, 1923, 1925, 1926, 1934, 1940, 1944, 1985
New reproductions copyright © The Estate of Cicely Mary Barker, 1990

ISBN 0 7232 4492 8

Colour reproduction by Saxon Photolitho Ltd, Norwich
Printed in Hong Kong by Imago Publishing Ltd

INTRODUCTION

Whether you have a large cottage garden or a tiny patio in the city,
gardening can be a relaxing, rewarding hobby. As well as providing
guidance on various aspects of horticulture, the *Flower Fairies Gardener's Year*
allows gardeners to note how their plants are performing, log the weather,
jot down the names of new plants to try, record orders of bulbs and seeds,
keep propagation records and plan for next year.

This book also features monthly reminders for jobs to be done in the
garden. The timing of these tasks is based on a moderate climate.
As plants may bloom earlier or later in warm or cold climates, it is
important to adjust your timing according to the climate where you live.
Weather and rainfall can vary substantially from year to year and should also be
taken into account. Every garden has its own unique climate, based on a
variety of environmental factors such as soil type and location.
By monitoring your garden in this attractive book, you can discover
which combination of plants is ideal for your garden.

CICELY MARY BARKER

Cicely Mary Barker, creator of the Flower Fairies, was born in 1895 in Croydon,
South London. Her artistic talent was evident from an early age and she achieved
international success with her magical little books. Painting directly from nature and
paying meticulous attention to detail, she went on many sketching holidays to draw
flowers. To achieve botanical accuracy in her illustrations, Cicely referred to
gardening books, clipped nature articles from newspapers and sent specimens to the
Royal Botanical Gardens for identification. This seasonal selection of her beautiful
watercolours will provide inspiration for gardeners throughout the year.

January

The Yew Fairy

Carefully fork over the surface soil around spring-flowering bulbs to loosen the soil and deter the growth of moss and weeds.

Dahlias   2002

In this dry year, the dahlias along the driveway were stunted. Needs much more compost there.

Sooter's Cupid — give more room

New this year - from Flower and Garden Show — Morgen ster — white ruffled. Didn't bloom.

Goldie Gull — Gold Anemone Dick Porter will give us for 2003. Prize winner at Dahlia Show.   *Good red ball: Riisa*

Put Honey Davenport in Inside, not by driveway.

Keep Murray Petit from getting leggy.

Dark Ball, Shadow Cat - need at least 2 plants

Hot Single — lost it.

Marge wants Fiesta back (salmon), Bright star, Honey Dav.? — *gave her none of the*

Linda likes Murray Petit, shadow Cat, Cheyenne , give Bobbie Sooter's Cupid.

MaryLou Valdez wants some yellow dahlias!

2003

New dahlias

plant size

1 Goldie Gull - from Dick Porter, Anemone, light blend of golds 5'

2 Riisa - miniature ball - red 3½'

3 Barbary Glamor - miniature ball, dark blend red/white 4'

4 Brush Strokes - Water Lily - Lavender

5 - 9 From Vicky at Jail (cell 410-0757)

England's Glory - purple/white

Hissy Fits - Yellow Fim

Masara - Pink/yellow

Red Cactus

> Apply a surface mulch to newly planted shrubs and trees. Firm the soil around these plants if they have been lifted by frost.

TREES AND SHRUBS

Woody stemmed plants originate from many parts of the world, giving us an enormous range of trees and shrubs to use in our gardens. Trees and shrubs form the framework of our gardens and provide beautiful shapes and sculptures. They can glow with colour or lend a subtle background to more flamboyant plantings. Apart from looking attractive and contributing colour, fruit and flowers in their season, trees and shrubs can also have fragrant flowers and leaves which add another pleasing dimension to the garden.

A mixed shrubbery, both evergreen and deciduous in various heights and widths, keeps the garden interesting throughout the year. In winter the strong outlines of the evergreens contrast well with the tracery of deciduous branches. The winter light catches the trunks and branches, highlighting their colours. New leaves on deciduous and evergreen plants provide a striking background to spring flower blossoms.

The shades of green available are extremely diverse. Leaves also come in a variety of textures, including those with fine ribs, some that are smooth and shiny, and others with a fine, suede-like feel to their undersides. This range of leaves in the evergreen trees and shrubs is multiplied again by the amazing shapes, textures and colours of the deciduous varieties. Add to this the multitude of textures, colours and appearances of tree bark and the possibilities seem infinite. This palette is so rich that a complete garden can be created with the foliage of trees and shrubs alone.

TREES AND SHRUBS

When choosing trees and shrubs for your garden,
research their ultimate height and spread, as well
as how many years it will take before they reach this
proportion. Some will eventually become large plants
and it is important to allow a tree or shrub the room to grow
and achieve its natural shape. Columnar, spreading, lollipop,
weeping and conical are some shapes which might suit a
particular situation.

Other factors to consider are whether the plant is deciduous
or evergreen, and whether it is dense with many branches or
light and open. These are important aspects to think about
when buying trees and shrubs, particularly if you have a small
garden when the shadows they throw can be heavy or a delicate tracery.
The shapes of the plants remain important even in winter. An evergreen
will throw a dense shadow of its shape, whereas a lightly branched deciduous
plant will allow light to shine through and only throw a lace-like
pattern. It is well-worth positioning a deciduous plant so that it
catches the morning or evening light and really glows.

You may decide upon a single tree or shrub which you will keep
pruned to the shape required because of its colour, flowers or
berries, giving it a place of pride in your garden. Whether or not
you have an exotic specimen, in a garden containing trees and
shrubs, interest can be maintained throughout the year with
foliage, texture and colour.

Feed established beds and borders with well-rotted manure. After digging and dressing the borders with fertilizer, apply a surface mulch.

<u>Glads</u>   2002

Got some new ones but the deer ate the flowers before they bloomed.

Put some in front garden but it was too dry.

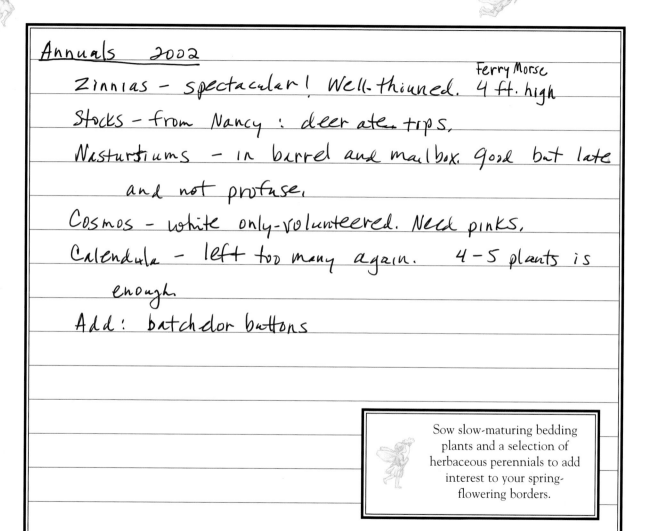

Annuals 2002

Zinnias - spectacular! Well-thinned. Ferry Morse 4 ft. high

Stocks - from Nancy : deer ate tips.

Nasturtiums - in barrel and mailbox. good but late
    and not profuse.

Cosmos - white only-volunteered. Need pinks.

Calendula - left too many again.   4 - 5 plants is
    enough.

Add: batchelor buttons

Sow slow-maturing bedding plants and a selection of herbaceous perennials to add interest to your spring-flowering borders.

February

Repair wooden support structures before plants begin to grow and re-lay loose or sunken stepping stones in the lawn.

Hanging Baskets   2002

6 baskets of ivy geraniums and bacopa did well but required much water. The blue lobelia was too hard to keep watered. The white petunias thrived, red too small. Bluish verbena was not showy enough, stopped blooming. I can't tell buds from spent blooms.

February

The Snowdrop Fairy

FEBRUARY

Provide plenty of food and
water for garden birds during
cold weather. If you have fish,
keep an area of your pond
ice-free so they can breathe.

Deck 2002

Impatiens did well in box. Chyrsanthemums with them are to big. Dark petunias in corner were good.

> Remove weeds that appear during mild spells and sprinkle slug bait among the plants. Position cloches to warm the soil for sowing in March.

BULBOUS PLANTS

The whiteness of snowdrops, resembling a late scattering of the snow through which they sometimes have to emerge, tells us that spring is on its way. Wild daffodils, their pale yellow trumpets caught by the wind but firm on their short stems, flower later and merge with the first bluebells. Heralding the arrival of summer, these rich blue bulbous plants will multiply and provide plenty of early interest once planted in a favourable situation.

Many bulbs are very suitable for growing in pots, which can be slipped into a space in the garden for their season and removed when they have finished flowering. This means that a variety of bulbs can be used throughout the year to enhance or change the surrounding colour scheme. It is well worth planting bulbs under deciduous shrubs, for the flowers will finish blooming before the shrubs' leaves have really established themselves. Give herbaceous borders a lift by painting them with a range of colours from the tulip family before the new growth of perennials begins. Mixed borders can also benefit from groups of tulips, narcissi and later, lilies, in colours chosen to enliven their background.

There are several varieties of alliums, some of which have upright, bell-like blooms and others which are pendulous in character. Yet others have spherical heads of closely packed flowers, which make quite a feature in beds or borders. The striking *Allium giganteum* has mauve heads which are held about 120 cm (4 feet) high in June. *Allium spaerocephalum* is about half that height, but looks attractive planted in groups. It flowers a little later with balls of purple crimson heads crowning its blue-green stems.

Bulbous Plants

Dahlias for late summer and autumn are valuable plants because of their variety of flower and colour. There are tall varieties which will probably require some sort of staking and small ones with a compact habit. Dahlias are suitable for the garden and containers and are useful for extending the garden's season of colour into the autumn.

To give the garden an extra dimension, it is worth searching for those plants with a fragrance. The hyacinth we know well as a plant which can be forced to induce spring in our homes early. An old favourite that is good for naturalising, *Narcissus poeticus* is a delightful single flower with a gentle scent. The Tazetta daffodil "Cheerfulness" has a delicious fragrance and pretty double creamy white flowers. On warm and overcast summer days, the Regale lily's fragrance resting on the air is memorable. Useful scented plants for later in the year are amaryllis and cyclamen. *Amaryllis belladonna* has bright pink, lily-like flowers growing in clusters on strong stalks. It likes a warm sheltered site and gives a sweet perfume. At the end of the year, *Cyclamen hederifolium* is worth growing for its beautifully marbled leaves and delicate flowers in shades from white through pink. Its subtle fragrance makes the winter more pleasurable.

MARCH

Plant out bulbs grown indoors
for Christmas in the garden.
They will flower again in a year
or two, after recovering from
being forced.

MARCH

Divide large clumps of border
perennials and replant. Harden
off and plant out greenhouse-
grown perennials when the
weather is mild.

SPRING

THE SCILLA FAIRY

Spring

Spring is a lovely season, bringing the promise of renewed life in plants and hibernating creatures. The lengthening days of spring and shafts of sunlight between bursts of rain encourage dormant plants to shoot forth. A hint of colour on the woodland floor assures us that the irresistible vista of the bluebells is almost with us. As the season progresses, the buds of early roses grow full and the cuckoo makes its first call to summer.

Perennials such as hemerocallis and peony, with tender new leaves in shades of lime green and bronzy red, look striking against a background of evergreen perennials and shrubs. The long, evergreen leaves of *Clematis armandii* make a stunning contrast to the scented, simple white flowers which look so beautiful with a clear blue sky behind. *Hamamelis mollis*, the witch hazel with yellow flowers, and *Lonicera fragrantissima*, with creamy white flowers, are other fragrant assets in the spring garden. Evergreen camellias with oval, shiny leaves and flowers from white through shades of pink and scarlet are good in the garden and in containers. Bulbs of early narcissus and crocus can cheer overcast days. This season is especially glorious when white cherry blossoms reflect dazzling light into the home, or when the sky turns a deep, metallic blue, making the new spring growth and blossom look intensely beautiful.

A busy season for gardeners, spring necessitates many jobs as the ground warms up. However, checking through borders, tidying up the winter damage, removing weeds, dividing and replacing perennials or planting new ones are pleasant tasks on warm spring days with the birds singing and the first butterflies emerging. Spring is the perfect time to try out exciting new combinations of plants and colours.

Plant climbers, such as wisteria
and clematis, allowing ample
space for their roots to spread
in rich soil. Wall climbers
should be kept well-watered.

Sow most bedding plants
indoors in a propagator. When
the soil has warmed up and is
neither too dry nor too wet,
sow hardy annuals outdoors.

Sprinkle egg shells or grit around plants to keep slugs at bay. Protect vulnerable plants from slugs by scattering comfrey leaves around them.

The Tulip Fairy

Dead-head tulips, daffodils, narcissi and hyacinths immediately after the flowers wither, so their energy can be put into forming new bulbs.

APRIL

Sow a new lawn or apply a nitrogen fertilizer to an existing lawn. Wait at least six weeks between bulbs flowering and mowing your lawn.

Container Gardening

For many people planting in containers is the only way that they can have a garden in the space available to them. A small area filled with plants in containers can become an exciting or tranquil spot with a little ingenuity and careful choice. A decorative pot chosen for a particular plant, or vice versa, becomes a special feature. The outline of the plant and the size of pot are important factors to consider, as are the handling of the container and contents for re-potting, and where it will fit into the scheme.

Almost anything from small to very large which can hold soil and enable plants to grow can be called a container. The choice of container is vast and largely depends upon the vessel's attractiveness and its practicality for the job. Traditional stone urns, vases, faux lead troughs, decorated or plain terracotta pots, baskets and wooden containers, old sinks, wire baskets, old hay racks, glazed pots and other man-made materials are all suitable for a contained garden. Large raised beds made from brick, stone or wood can enable planting at a higher level for ease of gardening or give the extra height required for screening.

Containers may require a liner made from a material suitable for keeping soil within bounds. Many liners allow plants to grow through holes made in them and some can be lifted out of their containers to allow for a change of flowering displays during the seasons. The final effect should not be spoilt by the visibility of the liner. Naturally, when small plants are placed in open-work containers, the liner will be on show until the plant grows and covers it.

Container Gardening

When choosing plants for a container, it is important to consider carefully the soil that they require. Always select a compost to suit the plant. For example, if you choose plants from the rhododendron, azalea and camellia families, look for a compost which is specifically for acid-loving plants.

By choosing different varieties of flowers and vegetables each year for colour and flavour, a contained garden can provide a great deal of pleasure in a small space. A decorative tree with colourful autumn foliage, evergreens or variegated plants in larger pots, with bright perennials, annuals and bulbs in smaller containers would give year-round interest. A small variety of fruit trees and seasonal vegetables in pots or other containers could produce an attractive area and fresh garden flavours for the table.

Planting in containers sometimes seems to mean a restricted view of gardening. This need not be the case. By utilising containers appropriate for the plants, by placing them on suitable bases or supports, or by securing them to a wall or fence, a garden of some height and depth can be achieved. A distinct advantage of this type of garden is that it is usually possible to change the design completely by rearranging the plants and containers whatever the time of year.

Apply organic mulch evenly to
rose beds to lock in moisture
and feed the plants. Hoe beds
regularly to remove new weeds
at once, while it is still easy.

Stake border perennials that need support to prevent wind damage. Complete staking before the plants grow to half their height or they will flop.

MAY

THE LILAC FAIRY

MAY

Remove dead-heads from
rhododendrons and lilacs as
soon as the flowers wither, to
prevent energy-wasting seed
pods from forming.

MAY

Purchase summer bedding plants or plant sown bedding plants outdoors. Water newly planted bedding and border plants during dry weather.

Lift dead spring-flowering bulbous plants out of their beds. When their foliage has died down, clean off soil and store the bulbs in a cool shed.

The Herbaceous Border

Perennials are the plants that fill our borders with summer colour. They are non-woody plants with a root base from which, each spring, new shoots appear and grow into flowering plants. Some plants' stems and foliage die right down during the dormant period, whilst other perennials retain a green foliage base. These useful plants, with their huge range of colours, varying heights and diverse shapes, provide gardeners with a rich and rewarding palette from which to design their herbaceous borders.

A traditional cottage garden would have had plants such as the pink near the path so that its rich perfume and dainty appearance would please each time it was passed. Peonies, delphiniums and phlox are some of the old-fashioned, well-loved plants which are still valued today for their variety of colours and distinctive shapes. In late Victorian times there was a fashion to have long, wide borders using perennials which could be left in the ground from year to year. As the clumps of plants grew larger, they were divided and placed in groups throughout the border. Walls were a useful background to a border, as were good green hedges and expanses of lawn. In large gardens, paved or grass walks would be bordered with deep beds of herbaceous plants. Borders would also be found in kitchen gardens, flanking the main cross paths.

Today, huge herbaceous borders are not to be found so frequently. The plants that were used in these borders, however, are still popular in a variety of schemes. Planted amongst shrubs and roses, with bulbs and in containers, they give an extra dimension of colour where gardeners do not have a great deal of time, but want the atmosphere of a colourful summer garden.

The Herbaceous Border

Creating even a small herbaceous border today can be very effective using large drifts of a single type plant of one colour, with a different plant of the same colour further along the bed. A mix of other plants and colours can be added to suit the design. The herbaceous border was designed and planted for colour, but whatever colour is chosen, green will predominate. It is therefore important to consider the colours of the perennial plants' leaves when planning the display. Look for leaves within the colour range you have chosen to add interest and texture. The heights of perennials vary from very tall to low ground cover plants and, skilfully woven together, can make waves of colour along the border.

Used imaginatively in containers, mixed borders or smaller beds on their own, perennials create a rich herbaceous atmosphere. Herbaceous perennials are also good for picking and flower arrangers can use the colourful flowers for decoration or include the seed heads in dried flower arrangements. Seed heads left in the garden look magical when their outlines sparkle with frost and also provide food for birds in winter.

MAY

Finish planting hanging baskets
and replace spring window
boxes with summer flowers.
Water container plants daily, as
they dry out quickly.

MAY

Thin annual and biennial seedlings sown outdoors to prevent crowding. If leaves on the seedlings are yellow, the plants may need to be fed.

ROSES

Synonymous with the rose is fragrance. The scent of the rose has been used since ancient times in perfumes and commands an extremely high price for even a small amount of essence. It has also been loved for its shape and colour through the centuries. As a token of love the rose is unrivalled through history, and even today rose petals are traditionally thrown at weddings.

Choosing a rose is a very personal decision. There are so many starting points. Roses offer a wide choice of appearance and perfume. It is important to select the right rose for the job required and to place it where its beauty can be fully appreciated. You should look for health, colour, fragrance and length of flowering, which will enable you to decide on the most suitable rose for your garden's situation.

The wild roses have a simplicity about them which is very attractive. Their gentle fragrance and pale colours herald the hips which flourish in the autumn. Hedges and wild areas benefit from their presence.

Shrub roses are useful because many of them repeat flower. They are strong plants and can make good hedges. This group of roses includes the rugosas and the hybrid musks, many of which also have hips.

Roses

When we talk of a rose's fragrance, it is often of the old roses that we are thinking. They flower once in the year, their petals ranging from white, through creamy pink, deep pink, mauve and crimson, and most have a rich fragrance.

Hybrid teas and floribunda roses, many of which are used in planting formal rose gardens, are modern roses. In this group of plants there are many colour variations and growers are always looking for something more exciting. Pale cream, apricot, orange and ginger brown are a range of colours particularly found in this group of roses. The hybrid teas generally have a single, large flower on a stem, whilst the floribundas have clusters of smaller flowers. Not all have a fragrance, but they do provide a long season of colour.

Climbers and ramblers are wonderful plants for giving colour and scent higher up in our gardens. Climbing roses usually have larger flowers than the rambler roses and generally repeat flower. When grown up into a tree or over an old building, these plants provide a wonderful waterfall of colour. Carefully trained horizontally across a wall or under the windows of a house, roses can be most attractive and, if scented, the fragrance will find its way through an open window.

Ground cover roses, which usually have more width than height, are very useful for difficult banks or to grow over walls and hang down. A variety with good disease resistance and a long flowering period can be a great help to a busy gardener.

JUNE

Regularly dead-head annuals
and border perennials to
improve their appearance,
extend the flowering season,
and give the plants more light.

Plant ground cover, such as heather, ivy or low-growing evergreens, which prevents new weeds from growing by blocking out sunlight.

Summer

Summer comes suddenly. One day it is spring, then instantaneously the next day everything seems to break into flower at once. Late frosts, which so often snatch away fresh magnolia flowers and decimate the young shoots of plants, are forgotten. The dazzling display that is a summer garden has arrived. Planting associations and colour schemes carefully thought out and planned in the winter months now prove themselves.

The colours of narcissi and tulips, so dominant in the spring garden, retreat for the performance of thrusting perennials and annuals. Pots, tubs and hanging baskets planted in the spring overflow, tumbling with brilliantly coloured annuals. Herbaceous borders full of promise now flower in waves of colour with the spikes of delphiniums as punctuation marks. Glorious roses in all shades bloom, their lovely flowers opening to allow their fragrance to scent the air. Mixed borders with flowering shrubs, roses, campanulas, catmint and geraniums are traditionally pleasing. Amongst all of this abundance and natural beauty, butterflies add to the colour and other insects hum in the exuberance of high summer.

Although a summer garden requires regular maintenance, there is plenty of time for enjoying lazy, al fresco lunches of salads and berries grown in the garden. When the light is waning on warm, late summer evenings and the pale flowers appear to float on their stems, there wafts the rich, evocative scent of the honeysuckle. This perfume reminds one that the flowers will soon fade to be replaced by berries and the sharp tang of autumn will scent the air.

Summer

The Pink Fairies

During droughts, leave grass clippings on the lawn to conserve moisture. Water the lawn once or twice per week in the early morning or evening.

JUNE

Keep your greenhouse
well-ventilated on hot summer
days and dampen down the
floors and surfaces to keep the
atmosphere moist.

July

The Candytuft Fairy

JULY

Continue to fight back weeds
with a combination of hoeing
and an application of a
weed-suppressing organic
mulch, such as chipped bark.

JULY

Visit other gardens to find
inspiration for your own
garden. Note down which of
your plants have and have not
performed well this year.

July

Keep wall climbers well-supported and continue tying in new shoots of vigorous climbers. Prune and feed summer-flowering climbers.

Annuals & Biennials

During the 19th century, the introduction of glasshouses enabled gardeners to produce masses of brightly coloured half-hardy annual plants for seasonal bedding out in elaborately curved or geometric beds. Spring beds would be cleared out when the flowering had given of its best so that the summer bedding could be planted out. This included annuals and biennials specially grown to produce dazzling displays of exotic-looking, vibrant blooms, which are still popular today.

The biennial and the hardy annual are extremely useful because they do not require the use of a greenhouse. In a traditional cottage garden, these plants are allowed to grow and make seeds, which are then collected and scattered where they are required to grow. Sometimes these plants just appear in parts of the garden where they have not been planted, nor would it appear to be ideal for the plant. Many seem to find suitable growing places for themselves between cracks in walls and paving, growing strongly and making fine plants.

All these useful plants can be planted to lend an extra puff of colour to shrub beds, mixed borders and containers. They are also useful for bare patches in the garden before other plants have time to fill out or flower, to extend a season of colour or to change a colour scheme. They look good in groups or sprinkled amongst other plants, providing a tapestry of colour such as you might find naturally on banks, in meadows and at the edge of woodland.

Annuals & Biennials

ANNUALS

These are plants which are sown, grown, flower and die within the same year. The seed can be collected for growing the following year.

Some annuals to grow:

Pot Marigold – *Calendula officinalis*

Shirley Poppy – *Papaver rhoeas*

Scabious – *Scabiosa atropurpurea*

Cornflower – *Centaurea cyanus*

Candytuft – *Iberis umbellata*

Love-in-a-mist – *Nigella damascena*

Sweet Pea – *Lathyrus odoratus*

Nasturtium – *Tropaeolum majus*

Larkspur – *Delphinium ambiguum*

Mignonette – *Reseda odorata*

HALF HARDY ANNUALS

This means that the seed should be protected in the early stages of its growth and should only be planted out when the danger of frost has passed.

Some half hardy annuals to grow:

Blanket Flower – *Gaillardia pulchella*

Morning Glory – *Ipomoea tricolor*

Tobacco Plant – *Nicotiana alata*

Petunia – *Petunia hybrida*

BIENNIALS

These are plants which are sown one year to flower the next.

Some biennials to grow:

Hollyhock – *Althaea rosea*

Snapdragon – *Antirrhinum majus*

Canterbury Bell – *Campanula medium*

Wallflower – *Cheiranthus cheiri*

Sweet William – *Dianthus barbatus*

Foxglove – *Digitalis purpurea*

JULY

Cut roses for use in flower
arrangements. Deadhead roses
unless the variety makes
attractive seed heads for
autumn interest.

JULY

Plant autumn-flowering bulbs, such as crocuses, for a colourful autumn display. Replace exhausted border plants with pot-grown annuals.

August

Pick sweet peas regularly to generate more growth. Tie in mature stems and cut tendrils on cordons. Water and mulch the plants in dry weather.

August

The Sweet Pea Fairies

To trap earwigs, fill inverted
flowerpots with hay or straw
and leave near infested plants.
Remove the flowerpots and
destroy the contents.

Arrange garden care, such as
lawn mowing, watering plants,
weeding beds and gathering
fruit if you will be away on
holiday this month.

FRUIT

The opportunity for growing fruit in our gardens today is enormous. There are now varieties of fruit trees which are grown on a smaller root stock and therefore require less room in which to grow. Because the trees are lower, the branches are easier to reach for pruning and picking. This has generated a greater interest in growing a variety of fruit in a small garden. Where there is enough space to grow a wide selection of fruit trees, it is possible to choose varieties which will produce a succession of fruit for eating, cooking and storage.

Pruning and training fruit trees is an ancient art. To create a design correctly, free-standing trees trained into shapes such as urns or cones require careful support in the early years. Espaliered trees are those grown on a central stem with branches opposite one another trained horizontally. Trees grown to branch out low down from the central stem and resemble a fan shape are known as fan-trained fruit trees. Cordons have a single stem, with branches pruned close to it, and are planted at a sloping angle. Because they can be planted closely together, cordons enable more varieties to be grown in a small space. All of these designs require careful annual pruning to maintain their decorative shape. Another method of training fruit trees uses canes to guide and shape the direction in which a wall or fence tree grows.

FRUIT

Whatever the size of garden, the vegetable area can be enhanced by using similar techniques of pruning and training some of the berry fruits. Blackcurrants, redcurrants and white currants respond well to being grown vertically up a wall or fence with only a few stems. Gooseberries can be treated in the same way and also look good grown on a longer stem topped with a ball-shaped bush. Growing these normally large plants enables the gardener to benefit from both a variety of fruit and a decorative garden. It also means that the plants are easy to reach for pruning and harvesting the fruit. Even more importantly, it is simpler to protect the fruit from the birds.

The small wild or alpine strawberry is an accommodating plant. It can be found flowering and fruiting in old gardens where the soil and site are to its liking. It can also be grown in pots, tubs and hanging baskets. Although its fruits are small, they have a delicious flavour.

Cane fruits are those such as raspberries. Each year, canes which have borne fruit must be cut out to allow new canes to grow for the next year. If space permits, the season of the raspberry can be prolonged by growing summer- and autumn-fruiting varieties. The blackberry is another valuable cane fruit which is often regarded as a prickly hedgerow plant, though one can grow thornless varieties which are easier to handle. Blackberries bring the promise of delicious pies to herald autumn.

Plant spring- and early summer-
flowering perennials for a good
first display. Sow hardy annuals
and plant young hardy
biennials for flowers next year.

Check whether any greenhouse repairs are needed before autumn comes. Fumigate the greenhouse and give it a thorough cleaning.

September

Lift tender perennials before the first frost. Cover summer bedding plants with layers of horticultural fleece if frost is being predicted.

The Michaelmas Daisy Fairy

September

Prepare the soil with bone meal, then plant bulbs for the spring and summer garden so that strong root systems can develop before winter frosts.

Prune off diseased or infested shoots of herbaceous plants and annuals. Do not put them in a compost heap, as that could cause more infection in spring.

The Mountain Ash Fairy

Autumn

The first frosts confirm that autumn truly has arrived. Dahlias, fuchsias and other less hardy plants become brown overnight and we have lost them for another year. Other plants settle down to begin their dormant season and start to lose their leaves. For some plants, autumn means a celebration of fiery colours.

During autumn, evergreen trees and shrubs must wait their turn in the wings. Their role in this season is to provide the supporting background. At this time of year, it is the deciduous plants whose leaves change colour and plants with berries and hips, such as bryony, hawthorn, privet and rowan, that hold the stage. Late-flowering perennials add their colours to the spectacle. Warm autumn days with sunlight making the colours of the leaves glow are very special. The rich reds, russets, golds and yellows of the leaves are echoed in the late border flowers. As the leaves fall, they gradually reveal views which have been lost behind the summer foliage. The fine tracery of branches reveals the sculpture of the bare trees and emphasises their graceful skeletal forms.

In days which seem to shorten quickly, there are less daylight hours to complete gardening jobs. Apples and pears are ready for harvesting, then storing or baking in pies and crumbles. Beds and borders require a final weeding before the onset of winter. The spreading of compost and manure is necessary to keep plants moist and nourished during harsh weather.

The sight of the pink *Cyclamen hederifolium* beginning to flower in sheltered places encourages our thoughts to stretch beyond the approaching winter to a new year. Indeed, autumn is a perfect time to begin planning next spring and summer's gardens.

Tidy away stakes and canes used for summer flowers. Soak the ends in wood preservative to reduce the risk of infection and make them last longer.

Plant conifers and evergreens so as to allow time for new roots to develop and provide the leaves with ample water during the winter months.

HEDGES

Hedges are plants used close together to form a barrier, a division or a decorative feature in the garden. Trees and shrubs are clipped from an early stage in their lives to produce a quantity of shoots which will grow into a well- meshed, good-looking hedge. Hedges are usually trimmed to a height and width which is less than they would normally grow. When planting or laying out your garden, remember to leave enough space to access your hedge easily for pruning without spoiling the plants in your beds and borders.

Evergreen hedges provide their colour year round. The choice is in the leaf colour, shape and texture. For example, yew has small, dark green, needle-like leaves, whereas laurel has large, shiny, oval leaves. Others, such as lavender, have grey leaves and the advantage of fragrant flowers. Most deciduous hedges lose all their leaves in the autumn. Some plants, such as beech, retain their leaves after they have changed to a honey-gold colour, adding an extra asset to a winter garden. Berberis and shrub roses make prickly, decorative informal hedges.

Blackthorn and hawthorn, traditionally used in country hedging, are other plants with sharp defences. Old field hedges consist of a mixed range of local country trees and shrubs allowed to grow for a few years. The stems are then partially cut through near the base and laid down along the line of the hedge. Stakes placed at intervals and a woven basket work finish to the top of the stakes complete this strong and impenetrable hedge. Field hedges also provide shelter and support to many wild flowers, such as Traveller's-joy, wild roses, Jack-by-the-hedge and primroses.

Hedges can be used in an imaginative and decorative way. They look spectacular when incorporated into an architectural or sculptural feature. A curved seat with a well-grown and cut hedge curving close behind it looks impressive. Hedges grown and clipped into sweeping or geometric shapes lend life and controlled movement to a garden.

A closely clipped hedge maze with constantly changing paths is intriguing, but needs careful planning to be effective. Smaller clipped mazes can be made with box or other low plants. The knot garden was created with various plants representing different strands of the design. You can add an air of intrigue by allowing some parts of the hedge to grow into an arch or window through which you can look into another part of the garden. Topiary shapes cut into the top of a hedge or as an accent feature can also be amusing.

Thinner hedges or screens can be formed with shrubs clipped and pruned close to their stems. Apple and pear cordons also make decorative see-through screens. Runner beans and sweet peas with nasturtiums planted amongst them can create a temporary summer screen with added culinary benefits.

Rake autumn leaves and use
them to make leafmould,
which will improve the
moisture, texture and drainage
of your garden soil.

Remove leaves from beds and borders to avoid snails and slugs. Clear dead herbaceous plants, but leave enough foliage to protect the crowns.

Plant windowboxes and hanging baskets to brighten up the winter months. Store any containers not being used in winter after disinfecting them.

The Dogwood Fairy

Prune deciduous shrubs and carry out any major cutting back required. Use spring-flowering plants to fill any gaps between shrubs.

November

Autumn is an ideal time to redesign your garden. Carry out measuring, marking and preliminary digging, but do not lay concrete in frosty weather.

The Beechnut Fairy

NOVEMBER

Lift tender bulbous plants, such as dahlias, when the leaves have been blacked by frost. Store the bulbs in a frost-free place, such as a cool shed.

Using sacking or netting, erect screens around small shrubs and trees of borderline hardiness to provide protection against strong winds.

Improve the pH level and structure of your soil, if the weather is mild enough, in time for the spring. Test your soil pH every two years or so.

WINTER

Even in the midst of winter, a garden can give pleasure. Though most plants are dormant during this season, there is still plenty of green to enliven the grey gloom. Evergreen trees and shrubs are valuable during the winter because they give structure, shape and colour to the garden. It is particularly at this time of year that one notices how many variations of green exist in plants. The conifer family includes plants with glaucous blue, grey-green and yellow leaves, and some that take on a bronze colouring when it is cold. The upright conifers make a very definite statement against a wintry sky whilst the horizontal varieties give a tiered effect and look wonderful with a sprinkling of frost or snow. Below them, groups of *Bergenia crassifolia*, whose leaves turn a mahogany colour, and *Bergenia purpurascens*, whose leaves change to a beetroot red, are good evergreen perennials. *Viburnum tinus*, an evergreen shrub which produces pale pink flowers through the colder months, is pretty, as are the small flowers of the deciduous tree, *Prunus subhirtella* "Autumnalis".

A real bonus in the winter garden is the discovery of flowers with fragrance. *Viburnum bodnantense* "Dawn" has fragrant pink flowers which are produced from late autumn to early spring. *Iris unguicularis*, the winter iris, likes a warm wall to nestle against in order to produce its silvery lavender flowers which are useful for a winter posy. Wintersweet, *Chimonanthus praecox*, also likes a warm wall and can scent a room with just one small sprig of blossom. *Mahonia japonica* has spiny tiers of leaves on top of which appear yellow flowers with a delicious lily-of-the-valley fragrance. A posy of these flowers for Christmas makes it seem as if spring is not too far away.

Winter

The Holly Fairy

Order or buy seeds as soon as possible, in order to provide a sufficient growing season for plants which are sown in mid or late winter.

December

Clear heavy snow off branches
to prevent them from
snapping. Take winter hanging
baskets under cover before
severe weather sets in.

Addresses

Name . . . .
Address . . . .
. . . .
Telephone . . . .

Name . . . .
Address . . . .
. . . .
Telephone . . . .

Name . . . .
Address . . . .
. . . .
Telephone . . . .

Name . . . .
Address . . . .
. . . .
Telephone . . . .

Name . . . .
Address . . . .
. . . .
Telephone . . . .

Name . . . .
Address . . . .
. . . .
Telephone . . . .

Name . . . .
Address . . . .
. . . .
Telephone . . . .

Name . . . .
Address . . . .
. . . .
Telephone . . . .

Addresses

Name . . . .
Address . . . .
. . . .
Telephone . . . .

Name . . . .
Address . . . .
. . . .
Telephone . . . .

Name . . . .
Address . . . .
. . . .
Telephone . . . .

Name . . . .
Address . . . .
. . . .
Telephone . . . .

Name . . . .
Address . . . .
. . . .
Telephone . . . .

Name . . . .
Address . . . .
. . . .
Telephone . . . .

Name . . . .
Address . . . .
. . . .
Telephone . . . .

Name . . . .
Address . . . .
. . . .
Telephone . . . .

ADDRESSES

NAME . . . .
ADDRESS . . . .

. . . .

TELEPHONE . . . .

NAME . . . .
ADDRESS . . . .

. . . .

TELEPHONE . . . .

NAME . . . .
ADDRESS . . . .

. . . .

TELEPHONE . . . .

NAME . . . .
ADDRESS . . . .

. . . .

TELEPHONE . . . .

NAME . . . .
ADDRESS . . . .

. . . .

TELEPHONE . . . .

NAME . . . .
ADDRESS . . . .

. . . .

TELEPHONE . . . .

NAME . . . .
ADDRESS . . . .

. . . .

TELEPHONE . . . .

NAME . . . .
ADDRESS . . . .

. . . .

TELEPHONE . . . .

Addresses

Name . . . .
Address . . . .
. . . .
. . . .
Telephone . . . .

Name . . . .
Address . . . .
. . . .
Telephone . . . .

Name . . . .
Address . . . .
. . . .
Telephone . . . .

Name . . . .
Address . . . .
. . . .
Telephone . . . .

Name . . . .
Address . . . .
. . . .
. . . .
Telephone . . . .

Name . . . .
Address . . . .
. . . .
Telephone . . . .

Name . . . .
Address . . . .
. . . .
Telephone . . . .

Name . . . .
Address . . . .
. . . .
Telephone . . . .

Addresses

Name . . . .
Address . . . .
. . . .
Telephone . . . .

Name . . . .
Address . . . .
. . . .
Telephone . . . .

Name . . . .
Address . . . .
. . . .
Telephone . . . .

Name . . . .
Address . . . .
. . . .
Telephone . . . .

Name . . . .
Address . . . .
. . . .
Telephone . . . .

Name . . . .
Address . . . .
. . . .
Telephone . . . .

Name . . . .
Address . . . .
. . . .
Telephone . . . .

Name . . . .
Address . . . .
. . . .
Telephone . . . .

Addresses

Name . . . .

Address . . . .

. . . .

Telephone . . . .

Name . . . .

Address . . . .

. . . .

Telephone . . . .

Name . . . .

Address . . . .

. . . .

Telephone . . . .

Name . . . .

Address . . . .

. . . .

Telephone . . . .

Name . . . .

Address . . . .

. . . .

Telephone . . . .

Name . . . .

Address . . . .

. . . .

Telephone . . . .

Name . . . .

Address . . . .

. . . .

Telephone . . . .

Name . . . .

Address . . . .

. . . .

Telephone . . . .

Addresses

Name . . . .

Address . . . .

. . . .

Telephone . . . .

Name . . . .

Address . . . .

. . . .

Telephone . . . .

Name . . . .

Address . . . .

. . . .

Telephone . . . .

Name . . . .

Address . . . .

. . . .

Telephone . . . .

Name . . . .

Address . . . .

. . . .

Telephone . . . .

Name . . . .

Address . . . .

. . . .

Telephone . . . .

Name . . . .

Address . . . .

. . . .

Telephone . . . .

Name . . . .

Address . . . .

. . . .

Telephone . . . .

ADDRESSES

Name . . . .
Address . . . .
. . . .
. . . .
Telephone . . . .

Name . . . .
Address . . . .
. . . .
. . . .
Telephone . . . .

Name . . . .
Address . . . .
. . . .
. . . .
Telephone . . . .

Name . . . .
Address . . . .
. . . .
. . . .
Telephone . . . .

Name . . . .
Address . . . .
. . . .
. . . .
Telephone . . . .

Name . . . .
Address . . . .
. . . .
. . . .
Telephone . . . .

Name . . . .
Address . . . .
. . . .
. . . .
Telephone . . . .

Name . . . .
Address . . . .
. . . .
. . . .
Telephone . . . .

GARDEN PLAN

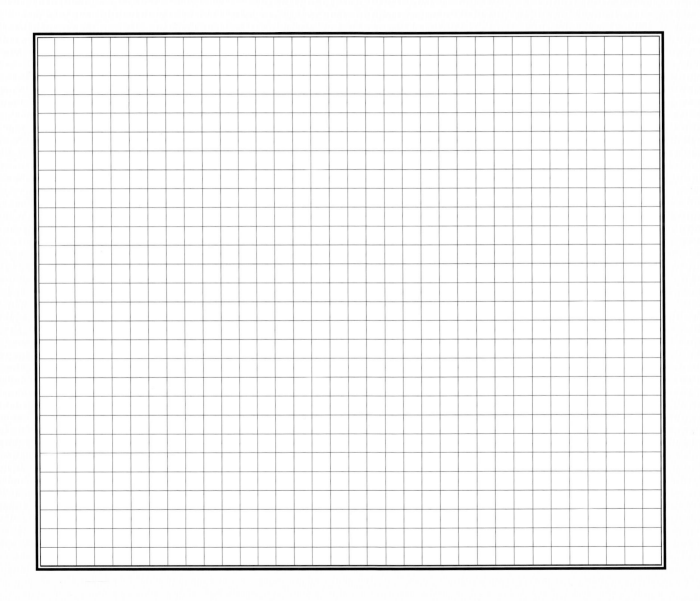

Garden Plan

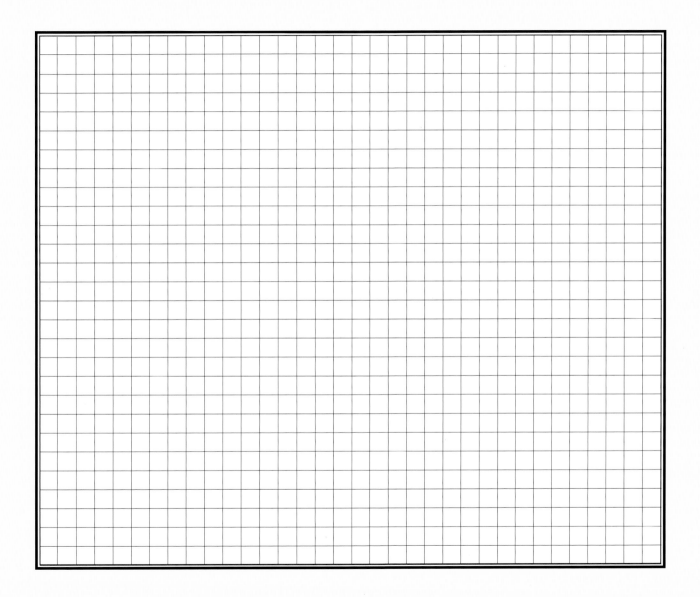

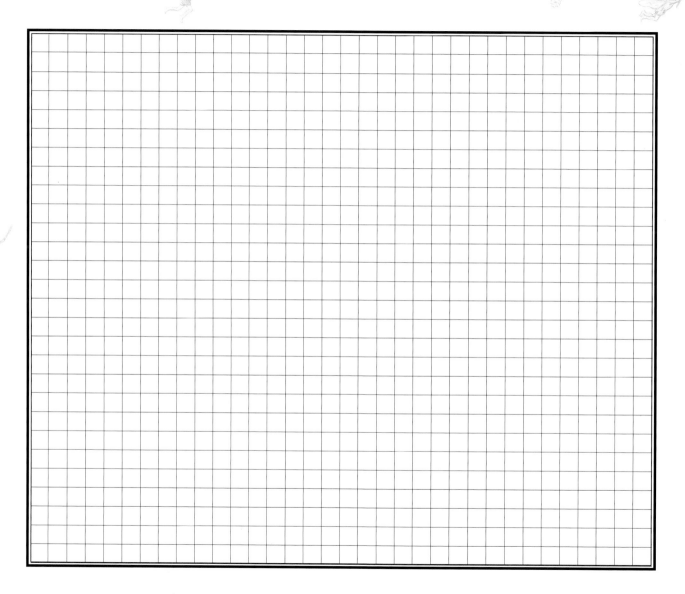

GARDEN PLAN

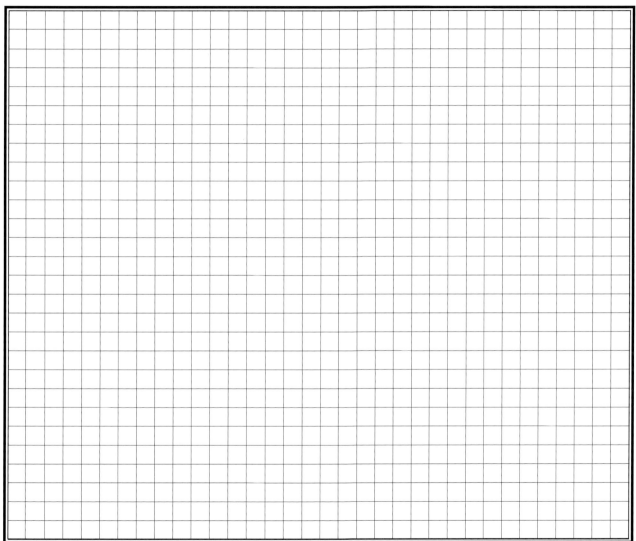

Garden Plan

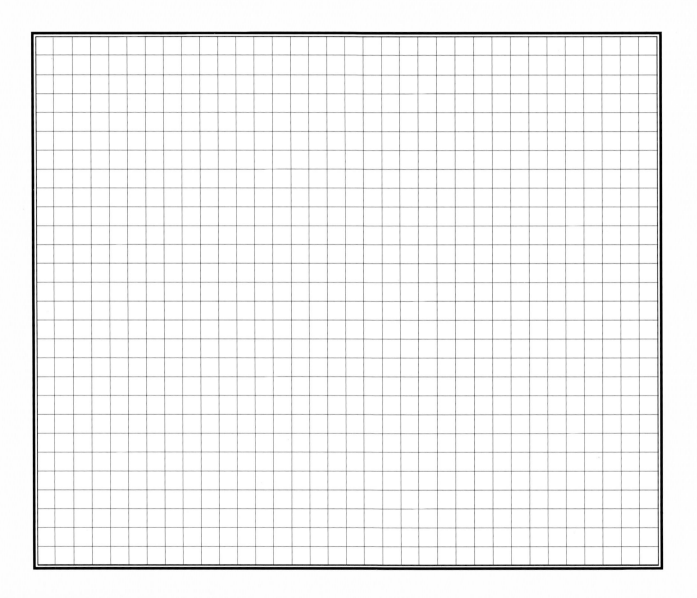

Garden Plan

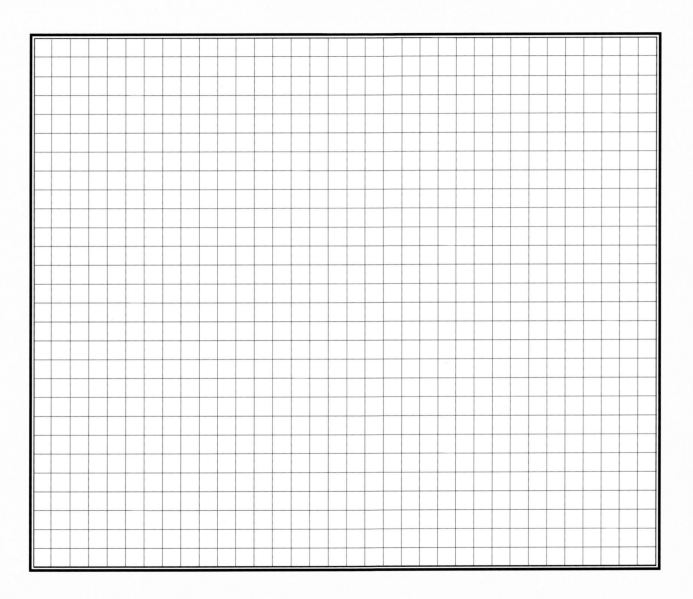

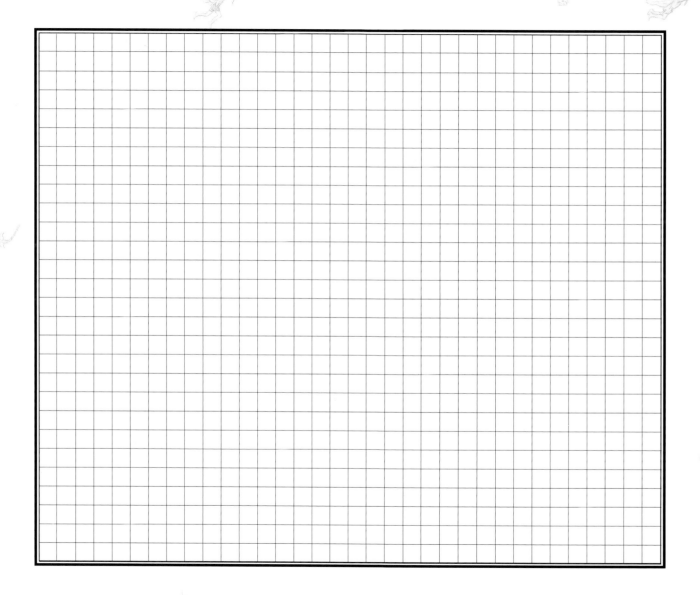

GARDEN PLAN

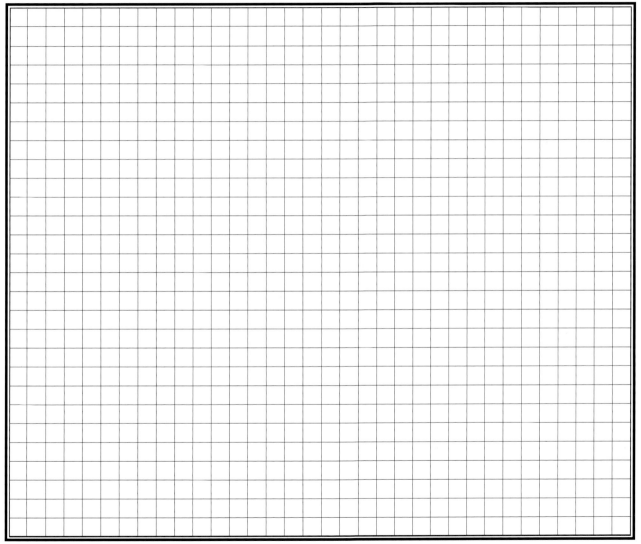

PHOTOGRAPHS OF THE GARDEN IN SPRING

Photographs of the Garden in Summer

PHOTOGRAPHS OF THE GARDEN IN AUTUMN

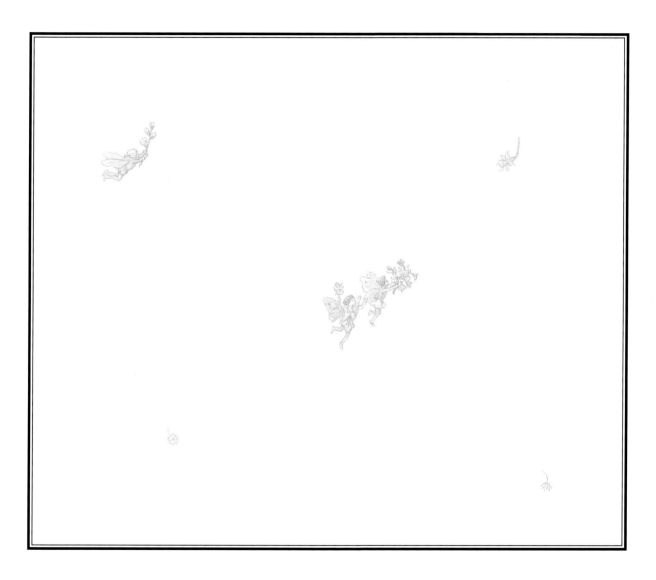